For Michael, Alessia, Thomas, Fido, Number 1, and Number 2, with love
—ST

For Rob. Your endless support means so much.
—CL

Library of Congress Cataloging-in-Publication data is on file with the publisher.

Text copyright © 2019 by Sue Tarsky
Illustrations copyright © 2019 by Claire Lordon
First published in the United States of America in 2019 by Albert Whitman & Company
ISBN 978-0-8075-7731-8

Printed in China
10 9 8 7 6 5 4 3 2 1 WKT 22 21 20 19 18

Design by Rick DeMonico

For more information about Albert Whitman & Company,
visit our website at www.albertwhitman.com.

100 Years of Albert Whitman & Company
Celebrate with us in 2019!

Taking a Walk

Summer at the Seashore

Sue Tarsky

illustrated by
Claire Lordon

Albert Whitman & Company
Chicago, Illinois

I went for a walk at the seashore today.
I saw lots of pretty little seashells.

Some of them looked like orange fans!

I went for a walk at the seashore today.

I saw pretty little seashells and one diving gray dolphin.

The dolphin was smiling at me!

I went for a walk at the seashore today.
I saw pretty little seashells, one diving gray dolphin,
and two striped beach umbrellas.

The beach umbrellas were shaped like triangles!

I went for a walk at the seashore today.

I saw pretty little seashells, one diving gray dolphin,

two striped beach umbrellas, and three leaping fishes.

The fishes splashed me!

I went for a walk at the seashore today.
I saw pretty little seashells, one diving gray dolphin,
two striped beach umbrellas, three leaping fishes,
and four big sandcastles.

The sandcastles had moats and turrets!

I went for a walk at the seashore today.

I saw pretty little seashells, one diving gray dolphin,

two striped beach umbrellas, three leaping fishes,

four big sandcastles, and five bouncing beach balls.

The balls rolled right to me!

I went for a walk at the seashore today.

I saw pretty little seashells, one diving gray dolphin,
two striped beach umbrellas, three leaping fishes,
four big sandcastles, five bouncing beach balls, and
six scuttling sand crabs.

The sand crabs were near a rock pool!

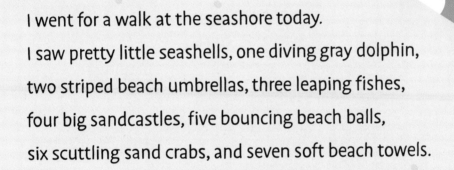

I went for a walk at the seashore today.

I saw pretty little seashells, one diving gray dolphin,

two striped beach umbrellas, three leaping fishes,

four big sandcastles, five bouncing beach balls,

six scuttling sand crabs, and seven soft beach towels.

The beach towels all had polka dots!

I went for a walk at the seashore today.

I saw pretty little seashells, one diving gray dolphin,

two striped beach umbrellas, three leaping fishes,

four big sandcastles, five bouncing beach balls,

six scuttling sand crabs, seven soft beach towels,

and eight large buckets.

The buckets had bright colors!

I went for a walk at the seashore today.

I saw pretty little seashells, one diving gray dolphin,

two striped beach umbrellas, three leaping fishes,

four big sandcastles, five bouncing beach balls,

six scuttling sand crabs, seven soft beach towels,

eight large buckets, and nine swooping seagulls.

The seagulls were squawking so loudly!

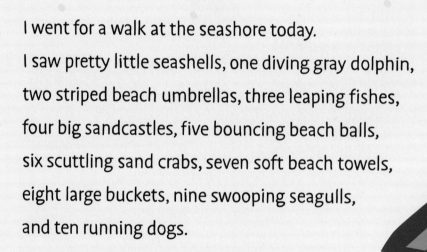

I went for a walk at the seashore today.

I saw pretty little seashells, one diving gray dolphin,

two striped beach umbrellas, three leaping fishes,

four big sandcastles, five bouncing beach balls,

six scuttling sand crabs, seven soft beach towels,

eight large buckets, nine swooping seagulls,

and ten running dogs.

The dogs were chasing each other!

I went for a walk on the seashore today. I saw

lots of pretty little seashells

1 diving gray dolphin

2 striped beach umbrellas

3 leaping fishes

4 big sandcastles

5 bouncing beach balls

6 scuttling sand crabs

7 soft beach towels

8 large buckets

9 swooping seagulls

and 10 running dogs.

What a good walk I had!

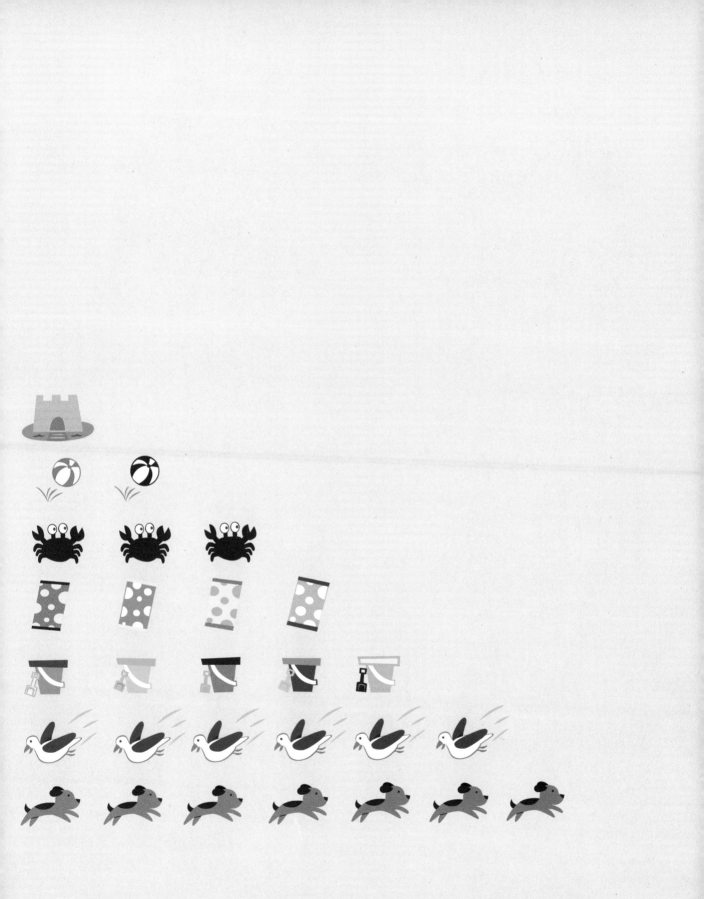